Love Next Door

Marie Hobbs

Copyright © 2022 by Marie Hobbs.

ISBN-13: 979-8-9872048-0-1 (paperback)

Printed in the United States of America.

MELODY'S LIFE is almost perfect. Graduate school, nursing, and now dating thanks to a good old-fashioned girlfriend's challenge. But what they don't know is Melody has already found the perfect man.

Miguel's the perfect neighbor. He checks the oil in Melody's car, hangs pictures on the walls, and handles the "Honey Do" List. But what he can't handle is another failed attempt at love, even though he thinks Melody is the perfect woman.

Two years as neighbors and friends is disrupted by a date (finally) gone right. Will Melody hold on to the dream that love is next door or move forward with a man willing and ready to give her forever?

Love Next Door

CHAPTER ONE

"Finally!" Kristen said, trying to hide her smile as she and Melody came out of the stairwell onto the fourth floor. The door closed behind them with a soft click.

"Oh, stop. It wasn't that bad." Melody flicked her hand dismissively.

A faint aroma of food wafted down the hall towards them. Melody turned in the direction of the delightful smells and inhaled. The savory bouquet confirmed she had made a good choice. A green sign with 1887 in orange indicated the popular new contemporary casual restaurant was at the end of the hall.

"This way," Melody said pointing to the sign. "And," she added as they walked, "you run the stadium stairs twice a week. Those few flights were not a hardship." She smiled at her friend and colleague.

"Maybe," Kristen partially conceded. "But this is a celebration dinner, not a fitness outing."

"What's wrong with multitasking?" She looped her arm with Kristen's.

Kristen chuckled lightly. "We certainly have done quite a bit of that in the past three months. All the extra hours putting together the grant proposal was a huge task on its own. But doing so while having to manage all of the activities associated with Thanksgiving, finals, the end of the fall semester, and Christmas break made it even more hectic. Then we jumped back in at the beginning of the spring semester to get buy-ins, sign-offs, and the proposal submitted by January thirty-first. It's been a lot." Kristen exhaled. "If I think about it too hard, I'll need to take a nap."

"Me too," Melody laughed. "So, let's enjoy some good food and toast our success."

Kristen leaned into Melody's shoulder and returned her smile. "I can get with that."

They arrived at 1887 about ten minutes before their reservation and checked in with the hostess. Not long afterward, they were seated and placing their drink orders. The ambient murmur of conversation, laughter, and the tinkling of silverware created a festive and pleasant atmosphere.

"I can't believe you were able to get a reservation so quickly. I heard there was a two-week wait," Kristen said looking around at the full dining room.

Melody smiled. "I made the reservation once I knew the deadline for filing the grant proposal. I knew we'd pull it off."

"I love it!" Kristen laughed and then raised her glass. "Here's to faith!"

Melody raised her glass in response. "To faith and the manifestation of it!"

"Now we wait for the Paladin Corporation to pick three finalists. They're supposed to announce them by May first. I think our health and wellness fair stands a really good chance," Kristen said.

Melody was an assistant nursing professor at Egglestead University School of Allied Health. When Kristen had shared her idea of a fair meant to educate the student body and the community on healthy lifestyle practices, Melody had gladly agreed to help plan and secure funding for it. The process had been rigorous, and the final verdict on funding was unknown. But Paladin would be remiss not to back such a worthy cause.

"So, do I. Well done, Dr. Harrison."

"I couldn't have done it without you, Dr. Martinez."

"Well, thank you. Maybe now that the proposal is done, you can invest more time in a relationship." Melody pitched her voice up on the last part of her sentence so it sounded like a question.

Kristen shook her head and smiled. "You're nothing if not consistent, Mel."

"I try."

"Yes, you do. So does Phoebe. But I'm done praying and hoping for a relationship." Kristen held up her hand when Melody opened her mouth to speak. "I know you mean well, but it's just not going to happen for me. I've come to accept that. I'm satisfied with my good life, career, family, and friends." Kristen gestured towards Melody.

"I thought the same thing."

Kristen drew her head back and looked at Melody in surprise. "You did? But you and Miguel have been married for 20 years."

Melody tilted her head to the side. "I never told you how Mig and I got together?"

CHAPTER TWO

22 Years Earlier...

"Melody, you're up this year," Sofia said.

Melody tightened her grip on her phone. It was New Year's Day and time for the Annual Girlfriend Challenge. Each year she and her three closest, long-time girlfriends – Shanice, Carmen, and Sofia – would issue a challenge to one of them. Not a solitary event or action, but a life change that would continue throughout the year. The purpose was to push her to grow, expand, and mature with the support of the sisterhood behind her. All those things sounded great when someone else had to do them. But this year was Melody's turn. Normally, she looked forward to a call with her girls. Not so much this one. She couldn't imagine what they were going to say. Thus, the sinking feeling in her stomach.

Melody swallowed and, with a slight tremble, said, "Okay."

"Girl, stop sounding like we're going to ask you to run into traffic on I-285," Shanice said.

Melody laughed and appreciated, once again, Shanice's ability to use humor to diffuse tension. "Well, that's a relief," Melody said releasing her breath.

"So," Carmen started, "we talked about it and agreed. Your challenge is to date."

Of course, they picked the worst possible task. Melody dived in with her usual excuses.

"You guys, come on. I'm in the last year and a half of my Ph.D. program and working PRN to keep my nursing skills up. I don't have time to date."

"Told you she would say that," Shanice said.

Melody huffed. "And besides, much to my mother's chagrin, I'm not sure there's a guy out there who's right for me. I'm focusing on having a fulfilling life with my career, my loving family, and my *amazing* friends." She didn't think the flattery would work, but she had to try.

"You're missing the point," Sofia said without acknowledging Melody's compliment. "Don't look for 'the one.' Just have fun."

"Like there's a long line of men in Atlanta waiting to ask me out," she countered.

"There is," Carmen said.

"What? No there's not. None of you live here. You don't know what it's like."

"Yes, we all live in different cities, but I have seen it, Mel. A man will be trying to get your attention, and you shut him down before he can even approach you," Sofia said.

"I do not," Melody insisted.

These women knew her better than anyone and they still didn't get it. But then it was hard to explain.

"Yeah, you do," Shanice added.

"*Es verdad*," Carmen agreed.

Melody huffed again and shook her head. Not that they could see it.

"Mel, just be open. Hang out with some new people. If nothing else, you'll broaden your horizons," Sofia said.

She didn't want to take a risk again. There were so many better things to put her energy toward – grad school, nursing, volunteer work. Things that wouldn't disappoint her. The last time she considered putting herself out there was two years ago when she first met Miguel. But he was very clear in wanting a friends-only relationship. And on top of that, she was busy.

"Or she could quit playing and date her cutie of a neighbor," Shanice suggested. Sofia and Carmen laughed. "You know I keep it real," Shanice added.

"Miguel and I are just friends. That's all. Nothing else."

After Miguel told her about his previous relationship, she understood his stance. To say that it ended ugly was an understatement. He'd been burned and was in no way interested in being in a romantic relationship again. If she'd been through half of what he'd dealt with, she wouldn't be either.

But at the end of the day, with all of her excuses, she didn't have a choice. Everyone else had stepped up. Sofia wrote and published the novel that had been knocking around in her head since college. Carmen submitted a proposal to be a speaker at her national industry conference and delivered a presentation that got her the exposure that her manager was trying to hinder. Shanice launched her own event planning business and was on a trajectory to be fully self-employed in a year. None of those had been easy, but each woman was in a better place in her life and career because of it. They'd started the challenges for their betterment, not their detriment.

Melody was bound by the oath of sisterhood to accept the challenge. And, boy, was this going to be a hard one. She swallowed and let out a long exhale.

"I accept the Challenge. Any suggestions on how to start?"

CHAPTER THREE

MIGUEL FLIPPED on his patio light, just as he had done almost every night for the past two years. He zipped his jacket and stepped out into the cold to wait for Melody. Her call with her girlfriends should have ended. She'd been a little nervous about what their challenge to her would be, but he had assured her that whatever it was she could more than handle it. He believed that. Melody was an amazing woman. And she was all his. *Sort of.*

Technically, they were just friends, but they spent most of their free time together. They would even fulfill the occasional plus-one duties for each other.

Even though it had been three years since the break-up with Celia, he was still recovering from it – emotionally and professionally. He would never put himself through that again. *Ever.* Even if it meant never having the family he always thought he would have. The risk was too great.

Melody's patio light flipped on, and she stuck her head out the door.

"*Mig, hace frio afuera! Ven adentro!*"

Miguel shook his head and chuckled. She *did not* like the cold. So, he wasn't at all surprised by her request to talk inside. He traversed the small patch of grass between their patios and stepped into her sunroom. She was on the love seat with her feet tucked under her, bundled up in the custom-made quilt he'd given her for her birthday the previous year. A space heater was on the floor going at full blast. He shed his jacket and took the chair closest to her.

"I should have dressed in layers." He pushed up the sleeves of his sweater and vigorously fanned himself with his hands.

Whatever," she said with an eye roll. "We're island people."

"Spain is not an island. Neither is Mexico." He loved teasing her. And she gave as good as she got.

"Keep it up, and I'll tell everyone you cried when we watched *Beaches*."

"Switching topics," he said quickly. "So, how'd it go?"

She released a heavy sigh and dropped her head. When she met his eyes again, she looked pained.

"I've been challenged to start dating."

Miguel struggled to keep his composure as his world turned upside down. *No, no, no, no, no! She belongs to me!* Her lips continued to move, presumably telling him more about the Challenge, but the buzzing in his ears drowned out all other sounds. He forced himself not to massage his temples to ease his throbbing head. *Maybe this is all a bad dream, and I'll wake up soon.*

"... not excited about it, but I have to do it. We have a code and an oath." Her voice penetrated the fog.

What are they? The mafia? Are they going to take her out for a drive in the desert if she doesn't do it?

He didn't want to risk giving away his distress by looking her in the eye, so he focused on the quilt. He'd had her favorite saying – *Let go and let God* – stitched on the center square. The rest of the patches were made up of memorabilia from her past and things they'd done together. He'd spent hours scouring eBay trying to find a t-shirt from her high school. It had taken months to gather all the items and weeks for the quilter to finish it. Now, she was wrapped up in *his* quilt talking about dating other guys. *No way!*

"You're my best friend in Atlanta, Miguel. You're gonna have to help me do this."

MELODY WATCHED MIGUEL CAREFULLY. Other than a slight widening of his eyes when she told him what the Challenge was, he didn't react. Just as she thought. Not even a hint of interest in her. What did her friends know? She held in the sigh that begged to escape. While she'd accepted the fact that they would only be friends, she'd never made the move to date anyone else. Had she been subconsciously hoping that he would one day change his mind? It didn't matter anymore. She had to move forward. For the first time, she began to think the Challenge was a good thing. Maybe she would meet a man like Miguel who was attracted to her. Yep, it was time to go all in.

"Well, will you?"

HELP HER? Miguel definitely *did not* want to help her find a man. But the only way to stop it was for him to speak up. The image of Celia straddling her personal trainer flashed before him. He flinched at the pain it brought to the surface. As if the infidelity hadn't been bad enough, he also had to fight all of the false accusations she made about him because he would not overlook her "brief moment of slumming," as she had put it. His heart clenched at the possibility of that type of betrayal happening again.

Miguel searched his mind for an answer. *What's most likely to happen? She hasn't met anyone in the two years I've known her. Maybe her dates will bomb, and this won't disrupt our dynamic at all.* Miguel nodded. *Yeah, I'm over-reacting. Let's just see what happens first.*

"Sure, Mel. Of course, anything for you. Oh, changing the subject again, I got that part for the toilet in your guest bathroom. I'll come over and fix it tomorrow."

"Thanks, Miggy. You're the best."

CHAPTER FOUR

"Four dates! Four dates in four weeks! And all of them disastrous!"

Miguel glanced at Melody from under the hood of her car. She was pacing beside it with her arms folded across her chest as her ponytail swayed vigorously. Her smooth, taupe skin glowed, and irritation blazed in her brown eyes. She was beautiful.

"Broaden my horizons!" Melody mocked Sofia's suggestion as she continued to rant. "To experience what, exactly? The guy from the gym whose girlfriend showed up in the middle of the date thanks to a GPS tracker she put on his car?"

She had already told him about three of the dates during their patio talks. But she was fired up and wanted to vent, so he didn't stop her.

"Well, at least you found out early on he was a

cheater." He kept his face hidden by the hood for two reasons. He knew she was shooting daggers at him, and he didn't want her to see the grin he was unable to hide.

"Miguel, not helping." She took a deep breath and started up again. "Or maybe the guy who two sips into my smoothie said we are destined to be together because we have the same initials."

Miguel placed the almost dead battery from her car on the ground and reached for the new one.

"Huh. That's an interesting theory."

"Yeah, especially since we don't have the same initials!" She exclaimed throwing up her hands.

He bit the inside of his cheek and began installing her battery.

"Then there was the guy from church – *from church* – who kept dropping innuendos, winking, and trying to grope me throughout the entire movie. Now, I have to avoid the bookstore when he's working."

Miguel bristled. She had left that part out of her recap the previous week. That brought him out from under the hood.

"Who was that, again?" He attempted nonchalance, but he was anything but. "Do I know him?" *Because he needs to know that he doesn't have the right to touch you!*

She waved it off. "Not the point, Miggy."

Melody was the only person he allowed to call him Miggy. He chose not to push the issue since she didn't plan to see that scumbag again.

"Fine. That was three. What about the fourth one?"

"That would be the guy Ashley in my grad school cohort set me up with. She's been telling me for months that she thought we'd hit it off. Well, he started with 'Wow, you're really pretty. I figured you'd be kind of homely since you needed to be fixed up. I'm glad I owed Ash a favor.'"

Miguel's mouth dropped open. He'd been out of the dating arena for three years, and even he knew that was lame.

She shook her head. "The first three all seemed so normal when we met. And Ashley raved about the fourth guy all the time." She released a heavy sigh. "This Challenge is ridiculous and wasting my time! I'm going to call a meeting with the crew. I can't keep doing this." She ran her hands over her shiny, jet-black hair. "Maybe it's me."

Melody was mad and frustrated. And Miguel couldn't be happier. The Challenge was going exactly as he'd hoped. While he was glad none of her dates had worked out, he didn't like the defeat he heard in her voice.

"It's not you, Mel. Trust me." He closed the hood of her car and wiped his hands on his shop cloth. "All done."

"Thank you, Miguel. You saved me time and money. As usual. You spoil me."

He shrugged off the compliment. "What's the use in having an engineer as a friend if he can't help every once in a while? By the way, your windshield wipers need to be replaced. I can get to that next week."

"Thanks," Melody said with a weak smile and dropped her gaze to the ground.

His gut clenched at the hint of sadness on her face. He tried to cheer her up.

"Hey, why don't you come over and watch the playoff game tonight? Javier will be here by then, and you know you like yelling at the television," he said with a smile.

She chuckled. "I do like that. And it'll be nice to finally meet Javier in person, but I'll let you two do your thing tonight and catch up with you guys tomorrow."

"Okay, but the invitation stands if you change your mind. You know where to find me," he said nodding toward his townhouse. The movement made his hair fall into his eyes.

"You need a haircut." She swept his hair off his forehead. His scalp tingled where her fingertips grazed it. "See you Sunday."

MELODY DECIDED NOT to hang out more for herself than for Miguel and Javier. To her surprise, finding dates hadn't been difficult. Mere days after she'd decided to be open and make a real effort to meet the Challenge, men came out of nowhere. Sofia's comment about her shutting men down before they had a chance came to her mind. Even if it was true, it was for the best. Evidenced by how bad the dates had been. She needed to figure out how to get out of the Challenge.

She stretched out on the couch and wrapped herself in the quilt Miguel had given her. But staring into space hoping for an answer to come to her wasn't working. As she absently fiddled with the gold cross that always hung around her neck, realization dawned. She bolted straight up and looked down. The words on her quilt leaped out at her. *Let go and let God. I jumped into the Challenge without even praying!*

"God, if it's Your will for me to do this Challenge, guide and direct me. Show me who to engage with and who to pass on. If it is not Your will, give me the words to say to Sofia, Carmen, and Shanice and prepare their hearts to receive them. Amen."

Sunday afternoon, Melody came to the end of her 5-mile loop around the subdivision before she knew it. Running cleared her mind and created space for her to hear from God. She'd changed her clothes after church, cued up her playlist, and hit the pavement. As she approached her mailbox, she saw a handsome man about her age taking luggage out of a car parked in Miguel's driveway.

"You must be Javier," she said as she took her earbuds out.

The family resemblance was most prominent in the ebony hair, deep brown eyes, and square jaw. Before she could tame the thought, she concluded that, while Javier was an attractive man, Miguel was more so.

"And you must be Melody. It's good to finally meet you," Javier said with a smile

"Same here."

He put the luggage down and walked to the foot of the driveway. "My cousin says you're joining us for dinner and football today."

"Yes, unless the two of you have other plans."

"No, no. Please still come. Miguel's making his world-famous paella. He uses Tia Maria's recipe. She won't give it to anyone else."

"Sounds delicious. I'll bring a salad." She looked down at herself. "After I shower and change."

"See you then."

MIGUEL MOVED AWAY from the window once Melody waved goodbye to Javier. Had Javier been flirting with her?

"*Primo, that's* Melody?" Javier asked as soon as he closed the front door.

"Yeah. Why?" Javier sounded a little too interested in Melody for him, but he would hear his cousin out before he reacted.

"Seriously?! Why are you not dating her? She is fine!"

"Looks aren't a reason to date someone. I learned that lesson, remember?"

"Why are you talking to me like I don't know you? You already said she's smart, God-fearing, and funny. Every time we talk, you're telling me about something else the two of you did together or something you did for her. And she's good-looking on top of all that?"

Miguel didn't respond. Instead, he went into the kitchen and started pulling out the ingredients for paella.

"No answer?"

He turned to face Javier. "Look. We're friends. That's it."

"I call BS," Javier challenged. He leaned on the back of the couch and folded his arms across his chest.

"If you don't believe me, you'll see at dinner tonight."

"Oh, I believe that you are 'just friends.'" He made air quotes. "My question is why."

CHAPTER FIVE

"Thanks for a fun night, gentlemen, but I have to get to bed. I picked up a shift at Cobb Hospital tomorrow," Melody said rising from the club chair.

Miguel and Javier stood as well.

"Thanks for coming over, Melody. I learned a lot." Javier shot a sideways glance at Miguel. "And hey, I wish you the best of luck with your Girlfriend Challenge."

Miguel's hands involuntarily clenched into fists. He quickly released them to hide his irritation.

Melody shook her head and smiled. "It has to get better, right?"

"Nowhere to go but up," Javier said laughing.

"I thought you were going to call it off," Miguel said as he walked her to the door. *Why did she change her mind?*

"Well, I may have been a bit hasty. I prayed about it, and I'm just going to –"

"Let go and let God," they said in unison.

She laughed. "Exactly. Good night, Miggy."

He returned to the great room and sat in the chair Melody had just vacated. It was still warm and had a faint scent of her perfume.

"You like her," Javier said.

"Yes, I tend to like people who are my friends," he responded, keeping his eyes fixed on the TV.

"I'm not talking about that kind of like and you know it."

Miguel sighed and let his head drop back on the chair. "And you're basing that on what?"

"You went to a musical with her."

He started to protest, but Javier continued before he could speak.

"Mig, you told your girlfriend of five years that you would not go to a musical with her even if she shot you between the eyes and dragged your lifeless body into the theater. You said you'd find a way to come back to life and run out screaming."

He didn't respond. It was just as well. Javier wasn't finished.

"You took an aerobics class and a yoga class. Guys don't do that unless they are trying to make their woman happy so their woman will make them happy later."

"You know, you have antiquated views about these things." He attempted a disapproving look.

"Yeah, and so do you. Which is how I know you like this woman."

He sighed again. "We are just friends, Javi."

"And it doesn't bother you that she's started going out with other guys?"

He hesitated. *How do I not lie without admitting the truth?*

"She has been given the challenge to date, and as her friend, I support her." He mentally patted himself on the back for his fabulous response.

"Uh-huh. You didn't answer the question. But since you are so supportive of your 'friend', you won't mind if I go out with her, will you?"

He recognized the wide grin on Javier's face. He'd seen it thousands of times through the years. His cousin was baiting him. They'd played this game before. His first move was to redirect.

"You? Are you saying you're interested in her?"

"In your own words, she's smart, funny, caring, down-to-earth, and pretty. Any hetero male who's not just a friend would be interested."

He scoffed. "Fine. But don't be surprised when she turns you down."

"Great. What's her number? Or you know what? I'll just walk over there," Javier said rising.

"No!" Miguel shouted as he bolted to his feet. He

hadn't meant to respond so vehemently. But the idea of Javier spending time alone with Melody forced a reaction beyond his control.

Javier froze, hovering over the seat with his hands braced on the arms of the recliner staring at his cousin.

Miguel cleared his throat and lowered his voice. "I mean, she may already be in bed."

Javier slowly eased himself back in the chair maintaining eye contact. Miguel grabbed Javier's phone off the coffee table and punched in numbers.

"Here," he said extending the phone to him.

"No time like the present." Javier took his phone and went to the front room.

She won't recognize the number so she won't answer. To his surprise, he heard Javier talking seconds later.

"Hi, Melody. This is Javier. I hope you don't mind that I got your number from Miguel."

There was a pause then laughter. *What's so funny?*

"I agree."

Agree to what? He strained to hear, but Javier's voice was muffled, so he could only make out snippets.

"... then how about at dinner tomorrow night? You pick the place."

Here comes the let-down.

"...7:00 work? ...reservation?"

Wait! She said yes?!?

"Okay. 7:30 then. I'll pick you up."

More laughter. *Whatever they are talking about cannot be that funny!*

"Okay. See you tomorrow. Bye." Javier had a satisfied look on his face when he came back. "And *that*, Cousin, is how it's done. Good night."

Javier went upstairs to the guest room leaving Miguel stewing.

MELODY HUNG up the phone smiling. This was great. Javier was the new regional director for a pharmaceutical company, and he wanted to bring in healthcare professionals to talk to his reps. And he had a budget to pay an honorarium. She had a stipend and made decent money picking up shifts, but every bit helped. Even better, his company was looking to partner with graduate programs to offer internships for nursing students interested in research or conducting clinical trials. She was beyond excited. She couldn't wait to talk more about it at dinner the next night.

MELODY SAT across from Javier at The Canoe Monday night. Their table was next to the floor-to-ceiling windows with a beautiful view of the Chattahoochee River. The lights strung from the patio railing reflected off the water giving off a warm glow.

"I'll reach out to your program director to get on her calendar for the latter part of the month. Things should be settled by then. Would you like dessert?" Javier asked signaling the waiter.

"It won't hurt to see what they have. How's the relocation going?" Melody asked.

"Pretty good. I found a place, but it'll be four weeks before it's ready. Until then, we're neighbors."

She put her hands on the table and leaned forward.

"I know this is a business dinner, but you and Miguel are cousins. Is it weird for us to be out together?"

"Not if you and Miguel are really just friends." He looked directly into her eyes and slightly lifted his eyebrows.

"Then it's not weird," she said with a shrug, dropping her gaze to the dessert menu.

"I think Miguel likes you, Mel, but he's ... hesitant to put himself out there because of his last relationship."

"Nah." She shook her head in disagreement. "I don't think so. We've been hanging out regularly for two years. We really are just friends."

"Haven't you heard all the friends-to-lovers stories?" He gave her a sly smile. She could only imagine the mischiefs he and Miguel got into when they were children.

She chuckled. "That only happens in rom-coms, Hallmark movies, and romance novels. None of which would I have pegged you to be a fan of."

Javier laughed. "I'm not. But my younger sister, Eliana, makes me watch chick flicks with her."

"Geez, the two of you are so retro," she said rolling her eyes.

"No disagreement here."

"So, wait. If you think he likes me, why are we out to dinner and not just meeting at the house or your office?"

"Well, for one, this is how I conduct business. I didn't want to short-change you because of familiarity. But concerning Miguel, I figure one of two things will happen. This will push him to admit his feelings, or it will confirm that he does only like you as a friend. For the record, my money's on the former."

"I hope you didn't put a lot of money on that. But if you did, I'll take that action."

He chuckled. "You're that sure?"

"Yes. I am," she said with a firm nod. Although, she admitted to herself, there had been a time that she wanted to be wrong. But the days of hoping Miguel would want to be more than friends were over. Now, thanks to her girlfriends she was open to meeting someone who was.

CHAPTER SIX

MIGUEL GAVE up trying to watch TV, read a book, or do anything other than wonder what Melody and Javier were doing. He sat up straight when he heard the key in the front door.

"*Hola, primo! Que pasa?*" Javier sauntered into the great room with a wide smile.

"Watching a movie," Miguel lied.

"Really, which one?"

"What does it matter?" he bit out. "How was your date?" He folded his arms across his chest and glared at his cousin.

"You seem upset," Javier said calmly.

"I'm not upset. I merely asked you how your evening was. Must have been great seeing you're just now getting home." He got up from the recliner and started pacing. "Which, by the way, is very inconsiderate. Maybe you don't need to be alert at work, but Melody does. She's in a very demanding graduate program, and she works as a nurse. You should have thought about that before keeping her out so late," he admonished.

"It's 9:30." Javier turned his wrist around so that his watch was facing Miguel. "You seem a bit on edge, Mig."

"If I'm on edge, it's because you haven't answered my question." He was barely keeping it together. Knowing Javier was goading him didn't make a difference. He couldn't reel it in.

Javier peered at him. "You look a little red. You know, that happens when you get angry. Have you noticed that before?"

He slowly turned to face Javier. If his cousin didn't start talking, Miguel was going to launch himself at his throat.

"I see you're hanging on by a thread, so I'll put you out of your misery. We had a wonderful time, thank you for asking. I'm going to see her again." Javier's grin grew even wider. "That is unless you don't want me to."

He didn't want him to. But he didn't want to admit it.

"All you have to say is 'Back off. She's mine.'"

Miguel looked at his cousin's smug face and grew more irritated by the second.

"I'm going to take your silence as your blessing. Good night." He turned to walk out of the room, but before he crossed the threshold, Miguel spoke.

"Javi."

"Yes?"

"Back off. She's mine."

Javier turned to face him. "Done."

The knot in Miguel's stomach and the vise that had been crushing his chest since Javier had left for the date both finally released. He flopped down on the sofa and dropped his head in his hands.

"For the record, it wasn't a date. It was a business meeting."

"Ugh! This is a complete disaster!" Miguel grasped handfuls of his hair in frustration.

Javier sat in the recliner. "Start from the beginning."

"When Mel moved in next door, I was still in the aftermath of the break-up with Celia."

"Things did get ugly," Javier said nodding. "I never thought she would retaliate by trying to ruin your career."

"Yeah. Fortunately, it was pretty easy to prove that she was lying. I was promoted to senior manager, but you know how it is with rumor and innuendo. That stuff follows you even after it's proven untrue. Some people love a scandal. Anyway, I decided I was done with relationships. I figured I could just have friends but no girlfriend, and definitely no wife," he explained.

Celia had been vicious enough in ending a dating relationship. He couldn't imagine how bad things would get having to divide assets.

"Then you met Melody."

"Yeah. And I liked her, but I was still determined to

stick to my plan. After a few weeks of waving and small talk, we were both out on our patios one evening and started having a real conversation. It became a nightly thing. When we had the previous relationship conversation, I didn't give her all the gory details but enough for her to know that things with Celia ended very badly. She hadn't dated in a while and wasn't really sure that she ever would meet anyone, but she had gotten okay with that. So, we started hanging out. A lot. All the time, really. I felt *safe*," he admitted.

"Safe?"

"Yeah. To say it aloud makes me sound like a jerk, but there was no competition. When she wasn't in class or at work or occasionally out with a girlfriend, she was with me. So, I could have her time and attention without having to risk anything."

Javier shook his head. "And then came the challenge."

He nodded. "Then came the challenge. I was concerned at first, but so far, the guys have been real duds."

"But what are you going to do when she meets someone great?"

Miguel dropped his head back on the couch. That was the million-dollar question. Unfortunately, he didn't have the answer.

~

Wednesday afternoon, Melody was nestled in the back corner of her favorite café working on the week's essay questions. She had a couple of hours before her next class, but she hadn't wanted to go home or stay on campus. Rev had been the perfect solution. They had good food, a wide beverage selection, and a strong internet connection. Most of the undergraduates sat up front so they could see and be seen through the large windows that faced the sidewalk. So, the back was quiet and much less populated. Perfect for a serious graduate student focused on her studies.

"Excuse me."

Melody jumped at the deep voice disrupting the afore-mentioned quiet.

"I'm so sorry," he said. "I didn't mean to startle you. I just need to share the outlet."

Melody looked up at the intruder. Her initial annoy-ance at being interrupted dissipated upon seeing his face. His chocolate brown eyes expressed his apology, as did his lopsided smile framed with dimples.

"It's fine. It's okay. I just didn't expect ... Usually, people don't come back here ... I mean, it's fine that you are ... It's not like this is a closed section or anything," Melody rambled. *What is wrong with me? He's just a man. A very attractive man with a lovely voice who smells like sandalwood, bergamot, and frankincense.*

"So then, you don't mind if I plug in? I promise not to disturb you. You looked so focused I didn't want to interrupt. But my laptop battery is starting to die." He lifted his eyebrows in question.

"I don't mind at all. Please." Melody gestured toward the outlet and then shifted to put some space between herself and the wall. If she was this thrown by his sight and scent, she might lose the ability to speak if he touched her.

He bent over and plugged in his cord. Then he stood and extended his hand. "I'm Jesse, by the way."

"Melody," she said shaking his hand. She felt a zing and held his gaze. The slight tremble in her cheeks alerted her that she was smiling hard. *I should probably let go of his hand. But it feels ... nice.*

Jesse's smile grew wider, and his eyes had a hopeful glint as they continued to shake hands longer than customary. He released her hand and cleared his throat.

"I'm going to sit over there," he said pointing to the adjacent booth. "And I'm going to keep my promise not to bother or distract you. But let me know when you're leaving so I can ask you out for Friday night."

CHAPTER SEVEN

MELODY FLIPPED through her date-worthy clothing options. She was meeting Jesse for dinner and a movie at 6:00. When he'd asked her out Wednesday at Rev, she'd been caught up in the excitement and romance of the moment and quickly accepted. But as she stood in her small walk-in closet and the time to leave drew closer, a feeling she couldn't quite define was nagging at her.

"Maybe I shouldn't go. Yes, Jesse is handsome and seems like a nice guy. But I thought the same thing about the others."

She took a royal purple sheath dress off the closet rod and held it up. Gold jewelry and low-heeled pumps would strike the perfect balance of not-too-casual but not-too-dressy. The corners of her mouth lifted in a smile.

"What is wrong with me? Of course, I should go! I accepted the challenge and decided to go all in. Even if this turns out to be another bad date, at least I'm trying. Right?" She looked at her collection of Beanie Babies, but they didn't answer.

Scenes from her previous four dates flipped through her mind as she dressed. Even though those had been complete flops and, from the outside, the date she was preparing for looked the same as those, it felt different. Nervous anticipation that she hadn't had with the others stirred inside her. She felt giddy, excited, and ... *guilty*.

"Guilty? Where did that come from? I have nothing to feel guilty about!" She stopped applying mascara and addressed her reflection in the mirror.

"Listen, we talked about this, remember? Yes, we thought Miguel felt the same way we did when we first met. But he doesn't, and we're moving on. Holding on to the dream that things might change is comfortable and easy. And it gives us an excuse to stay the same. But it's also holding us back from experiencing life to the fullest. Granted none of the dates so far have been home runs, but even Jackie Robinson and Hank Aaron struck out sometimes."

She finished her make-up and gave herself a once-over.

"Not bad if I do say so myself."

As she turned to leave, she looked over at the window facing Miguel's patio and debated whether to tell him she wouldn't be meeting him later. Her stomach fluttered.

"He'll have a bunch of questions." She glanced at her watch. "And it'll make me late. And that would be rude.

As much as tardiness in others irritates me, how can I be late? I'll tell him tomorrow. No big deal."

MIGUEL CALLED Melody for the tenth time in the fifteen minutes he had been waiting for her to come out on her patio Friday night. Like the others before, it went straight to voicemail. He checked again for a text or voicemail message from her. Nothing. *She's probably in the library. No need to worry. It's not the first Friday night she's spent studying.* But it was the first time she had done so without letting him know.

THE NEXT AFTERNOON, Melody stretched out on the couch with the phone to her ear and a wide grin on her face as she finished telling the crew about meeting Jesse on Wednesday and their date the night before. For a few moments, they were silent. Then they all spoke at once.

"Yes! See what prayer will do?" Shanice exclaimed.

"I'm so happy for you!" Sofia shouted.

"*¡Aleluya!*" Carmen cried out with joy.

Then their voices became a jumble of Spanish and English. Melody couldn't make out anything being said.

"Hold on. I know we are all excited for Mel, but we can't all talk at once," Sofia said.

Melody heard typing, then Shanice spoke.

"You're not going to believe this! The name Jesse means God's gift!"

"Does it really?" Melody asked. It wasn't lost on her that she met Jesse just three days after she prayed about the Challenge. *Could he be God's gift to me?*

"Wow!" Sofia and Carmen whispered in unison.

"So, what's next?" Carmen asked.

"We're getting together this evening," Melody said.

"Best monthly check-in ever!" Shanice said, and the others agreed.

MELODY SLOWLY WALKED to Miguel's house. She admitted to herself that she was stalling because she was nervous. But that didn't make sense. Seeing Miguel had never made her nervous before. And she still didn't know why she didn't just tell him about her date with Jesse the day before. She'd told him about all the others. Why was this one different? Too many unusual feelings. Too many unanswered questions. She didn't like it at all. But she was determined to do what she should have done on Wednesday. If he really was her best friend in Atlanta like she always claimed, she had to tell him.

Javier opened the door after she rang the bell.

"You, young lady, have some 'splainin' to do," he said, wagging his finger at her.

She laughed and stepped inside. "I'm sure I do. Is Mig home?"

He nodded. "Yep, he's in his office. I, on the other hand, am heading out. So, I cannot be called as a witness for either side."

She laughed again. "You're so dramatic. You sure you're in sales and not acting?"

"Basically, the same thing," he said with a shrug. "See you later."

She waited until she heard his car start before going to Miguel's office. She found him staring intently at his computer screen typing. He was in a zone. He could block out the world when he was working on a problem. She wasn't sure he even knew she was there until he spoke.

"Glad to see you're okay." He didn't look at her or stop typing.

"Yeah, sorry about that. I should've told you I was going to miss our talk last night."

He stopped typing and looked at her with tired eyes. "Mel, I get that you're in the last year and a half of your program. You'll probably have to pull all-nighters in the library a lot. Just let me know, as your friend, that you're okay. I know you can take care of yourself, but you're a single woman in a large city late at night. Someone should know where you are." He resumed typing.

She dropped her gaze to the floor. It was time to woman up and tell him. "I ... I wasn't at the library." She looked up at him. "I was on a date."

He snapped his head around to face her, but his eyes were unreadable. "Oh?"

"Yeah, his name is Jesse, and –"

"You can tell me all about it tonight," he interrupted. "I need to finish this up. Your place or mine?"

"Ah, about that," she said slowly. "We're getting together again this evening, so I won't be able to –"

"That's fine," he said quickly, interrupting again. "We can talk whenever. Or not at all. Whatever." He turned away from her and started typing again.

"Mig." He didn't answer. "Mig, come on! You're one of my best friends."

"Am I?" His words dripped with disdain.

"Seriously? I mess up one time, and we're not friends anymore?" She asked in disbelief.

He sighed and dropped his head, then he got up from his desk and stood in front of her. "You're right. I'm sorry. This project at work has me on edge," he said sincerely.

"So, we're good?" She looked up into his deep brown eyes, and out of nowhere she thought, *Mig's eyes are nicer than Jesse's.*

"Yeah, we're good." He pulled her into a quick, platonic, just-a-friend hug. "Now get outta here! I have work to do and you have to get ready for your date."

"Thanks, Miggy. Bye."

Miguel waited for a full minute after he heard the front door close before he flopped back in his chair and let out the growl that had been lodged in his throat since Melody had said the word "date." He shook his fists and then pressed his hands to his face as jealousy stirred inside him. He needed something to hit or throw.

"Yep. This is a disaster."

CHAPTER EIGHT

"Hey, Shani. What's up?" Melody answered her phone.

"Just calling to check on you, girl. Are you getting ready for your date?"

Melody sighed and lay across the bed. "I'm trying to decide what to wear."

She needed to talk about what had happened with Miguel. If she could talk to anyone, it was Shanice.

"I told Miguel I was out on a date last night. And the conversation got weird for a minute."

Shanice was silent for a few beats. "He didn't know? I thought you told him about all your dates."

"I had up until yesterday," she admitted.

"Why not?"

Melody hesitated. How could she explain it to Shanice without her reading more into it?

"I ... I didn't think about it until I was about to walk out of the door. I was concerned about being late, so I just decided to wait and tell him today."

She squeezed her eyes shut and waited for Shanice to dismantle her argument. She could have texted him. She could have called him from the car. She could have told him during their patio talk on Wednesday or Thursday.

"Hmm," Shanice said thoughtfully. "The conversation got weird how?"

"Well, he was okay when he thought I was a no-show because I was in the library. But when I told him I was on a date, he questioned our friendship."

"Hmm," Shanice said again.

"But then he apologized. He's a little stressed about work, so I think he just needed to blow off some steam," she quickly explained.

"I think he likes you," Shanice stated bluntly.

Only Shanice knew she had been attracted to Miguel when they first met. And that she'd thought it was mutual until Miguel made his friends-only intentions known.

Melody chuckled. "You realize that we've had this conversation at least 10 times over the past two years, right? Nothing has changed. We're friends. That's the way we both want it." She involuntarily flinched at the last sentence. She chose not to consider why.

"Doesn't mean he doesn't like you," Shanice countered.

"Shani ..."

"Mel, the man fixed your toilet. Your *toilet*!"

She sat up crossed-legged on the bed.

"Okay. For the sake of argument, let's say that he does like me as more than a friend. It's irrelevant."

"Irrelevant? Why?"

"Because he made the decision to just be friends for a reason, and that reason has not changed or gone away."

"And there has never been anything between you?"

She thought back to the little sister hug Miguel gave her earlier. "No."

"Never? Late at night? On the patio? Snuggled on the sofa watching a movie?" Shanice asked in a sing-song voice.

"For the record, we have never snuggled," she said lightly laughing. "But no. Never."

"No kiss? Not even on the cheek?" Shanice asked in disbelief.

"No. Nothing."

"Huh. You may be right," Shanice said then quickly added, "but I still don't think this story is over."

MELODY SMILED across the table at Jesse the following Tuesday afternoon as their lunch plates were cleared and replaced with dessert menus.

"That was delicious," Jesse said, returning her smile. "Good call." He glanced at his watch. "And good timing."

Jesse had a clinical instruction session for Year 3 Doctor of Physical Therapy students at the hospital in twenty minutes. Melody's next class was starting in thirty minutes. Abbott's sat in the middle of the hospital-university complex and was one of two restaurants where you could have a sit-down meal and finish in an hour.

"Abbott's never disappoints," she agreed.

He shifted in his chair and then looked her in the eye.

"Melody, will you be my valentine?" His eyes glistened with hope.

They had talked every day since they met and had seen each other four of those seven days. But it felt like she'd known him for much longer. There was a connection.

"Well, that depends on what you mean."

He reached across the table and put his hand on top of hers.

"I realize we've only known each other for a short time, but this feels real. I'm not interested in a casual relationship, Melody. I'm 30 years old. I want to be with someone I can have a future with."

"Jesse, I –"

"You don't have to answer me right now. I've prayed about us. I want you to pray about us, too. And if this," he gestured between them, "or I am not who or what you want, I would rather know now than months down the road."

She took in the man in front of her. He was clear on

what he wanted and told her directly, and that made him even more attractive.

"I will, Jesse. And I'll have an answer before Valentine's Day on Monday."

MIGUEL LOOKED up at his office ceiling as he reclined on the lounge chair and ottoman that Melody had helped him pick out. He was supposed to be working from home, but he couldn't stop thinking about Melody's dates with Jesse. Javier was out meeting with reps and calling on hospitals, so there was nothing to pull him away from his thoughts.

Melody was on campus and "staying in the area" until she was done with all her classes and meetings. Tuesday was a full day for her, but she usually came home for a few hours around lunchtime.

Was she with that Jesse guy again?

If she was and she was happy, shouldn't he just let her be happy? Wasn't that what a friend would do? Could he take the risk to be more than friends?

Melody was not Celia. But nothing in the five years with Celia suggested that she would cheat and then become vindictive. How could he be sure Melody wouldn't betray him, too?

Maybe this Jesse guy is best for her. His heart screamed *"No!"* before he could even finish the thought. He was going to have to … The phone rang interrupting his thoughts.

"Hello?"

"Good morning. May I speak with Miguel Martinez, please?" an unknown male voice said.

"This is he." Miguel prepared himself to hang up on yet another telemarketer.

"Mr. Martinez, this is Dwayne, personal assistant to Celia Darrington."

Miguel shook his head. *Really? A personal assistant?*

"She would like to meet with you at your earliest convenience."

"That's not possible. I'm very busy." Even if he wasn't, the last person he wanted to see was Celia.

"It's very important, Mr. Martinez. 'Imperative' was her exact word. Ms. Darrington will rearrange her schedule in any way necessary to accommodate you."

Miguel sighed. *Maybe she wants to apologize. If I hear her out, it might be what I need to finally move on. I'm tired of the break-up hanging over me.*

"Fine." Miguel glanced at his watch. "How about a late lunch at Abbott's?"

MELODY WALKED OUT OF THE LADIES' room thinking about Jesse's question. He was a gentleman, funny, kind, attentive, and very easy on the eyes. And she liked him. She felt good when she was with him. But was it too soon to start dating exclusively? Did she know him well enough to decide that? Despite trying not to, she wondered how a relationship with Jesse would affect her relationship, er *friend*ship, with Miguel.

She turned left to head back to the table and saw Miguel coming through the front door. Initially, she was concerned about him seeing her with Jesse. But that was short-lived.

As soon as he was fully inside the restaurant, a woman with a modelesque face, a pin-up girl body, and thick, wavy, chestnut hair down to her mid-back walked up to Miguel and hugged him. A full-body contact hug. The complete opposite of the hug Miguel had given her on Saturday. The woman looped her arm with Miguel's, then they followed the hostess to be seated.

Melody went completely still, except for her eyes which blinked in rapid succession. Her brain stalled for a few moments then jerked into gear processing what she had seen. Miguel wasn't on a dating hiatus. He just wasn't interested in dating her.

CHAPTER NINE

GETTING BACK to the table was like walking through water against the current. Melody must have looked as stricken as she felt. Jesse peered at her with concern as she took her seat.

"Are you okay"? He reached across the table and took her hand.

She nodded. "I'm fine. I just saw my neighbor."

"Miguel, right?" Jesse asked.

She nodded again. He looked pleased that he'd remembered Miguel's name.

"Should we go over and say 'hi'"?

"No. I think ... I think he's on a date," Melody managed to say.

"Then you're right. We shouldn't disturb them."

MIGUEL WAS glad to be seated and have some distance between him and Celia. He had to practically pry her fingers off his arm when they got to the table. He was starting to think this was a bad idea.

"Okay, Celia, I'm here. What's so important that you had your assistant set up this meeting?" he asked getting straight to the point.

"Celia? Not CeCe?" she asked sweetly while batting her eyes at him.

He didn't respond. She sighed dramatically.

"Well, I've been thinking a lot lately about what happened between us." She leaned in, placing well-manicured hands on the table. "We let things get out of hand."

"We?"

"Fine. *I* let things get out of hand, Michael."

"Miguel," he said firmly.

"You used to let me call you Michael sometimes." She batted her eyes again. He couldn't believe that used to work on him.

"That was a long time ago, Celia."

"Not so long that I don't remember how good we were together." She reached across the table. He put his hands on his lap.

"Until you decided to be 'good' with another guy."

"A mere dalliance," she said with a flick of her wrist.

"It was more than that to me."

"I know. And I'm sorry. And I behaved badly afterward. I'm sorry for that, too." She twirled a clump of her hair around her finger and tried to look penitent.

"Behaved badly? Celia, you tried to get me fired by falsely accusing me of an ethics violation." He controlled his voice, but he was roiling inside.

"I was desperate. I didn't want to lose you."

"So, you thought ruining my career would win me back?" he asked in utter disbelief.

"Admittedly not one of my best moments," she responded flippantly.

He lost his battle to keep his expression neutral. His eyes widened, and his mouth fell open, but no words would come out. It wouldn't have made a difference if they had. Celia was still Celia. Only concerned about getting what she wanted. No matter who got trampled in the process. He looked around the restaurant to focus on anything but her.

"Miguel," she said slowly and sweetly, "I think we should get back together. Enough time has passed since those unfortunate events occurred. We're 30 and more mature now. Indiscretions from our twenties shouldn't hold us back in our lives today."

At that moment, his eyes settled on something. Melody was leaving the restaurant with a man who had his hand possessively at the small of her back.

"Miguel? Miguel, did you hear me?" Celia asked.

He shook his head and then immediately regretted it. It was still pounding from the blood rushing through his ears. He wasn't sure whether it was anger, jealousy, or a combination. It didn't matter. He knew what he had to do.

"Celia, you're right." She sat up straight and smiled brightly. "We shouldn't let things from our twenties hinder us today. I've been letting what you did stop me from pursuing the life and the person I want. But that ends today. Thank you for meeting with me. It's been liberating."

Miguel got up from the table and walked out the door.

"Hi, neighbor."

Melody heard Javier's voice behind her as she walked to her car after the meeting with her advisor. Students, professors, hospital staff, visitors, shoppers, and restaurant patrons all used the large parking lot and adjacent deck in the center of the complex. If you scored a spot there, you didn't move your car until you were leaving for the day. She turned and stopped on the sidewalk to let Javier catch up with her.

"Were you here for meetings?" she asked.

"Yes. One of my reps was calling on the pharmacy director at the hospital. You done for the day?"

"Yes, finally. Are you parked in the lot?"

"Yep. Let's head out." He tilted his head toward the lot.

They had been walking and chatting for about five minutes when they heard a woman behind them say, "Javier Martinez."

Melody turned around to see the woman who was with Miguel at lunch walking toward them. She moved in to hug Javier, but he stepped back. She laughed off his rejection and then turned to Melody.

"Oh, I hope I'm not interrupting anything." She looked between Melody and Javier a few times then extended her hand to Melody.

"Celia Darrington. Don't mind Javier and me. I'm a friend of the family."

Melody's stomach dropped to her feet. Though she'd never seen a picture, she knew the name of Miguel's ex. And from the looks of them at lunch, she was about to be his ex-ex.

"Melody Correra." She forced herself to shake Celia's hand and smile. She hoped it didn't look as fake as it felt.

"Celia, nice to meet you," she lied. "But it's been a long day. Please excuse me. Javier, we'll catch up later."

Melody walked away as quickly as she could to her car.

CHAPTER TEN

MIGUEL WAS in his home office when Javier came through the door.

"Why was Celia at the hospital-university complex today?" Javier called out.

"Long story short, she wanted to get back together," Miguel answered while walking down the hall.

When he didn't get a response, he called out. "Javi? Javi, did you hear me?"

At the end of the hall, Javier stood motionless with bugged-out eyes and mouth hanging open.

"That's the same look I had." He walked past him to the kitchen.

"She what?!"

Miguel dismissed the question with a wave and opened the refrigerator. "That's not the most important thing that happened at lunch today."

"It's not?" Javier asked in disbelief.

"No. I saw Mel leaving Abbott's with who must have been that Jesse guy and his hands were all over her!"

To some that may have been an exaggeration, but that was what it looked like to him.

"Bad news: Mel and I were walking to the parking lot when we ran into Celia."

Miguel coughed up the water he was drinking. "Please tell me you're not serious," he said with a raspy voice.

"Lo siento, primo. Es verdad."

He dropped down on the sofa and covered his face with his hands. "This Jesse," he spat out, "is clearly trying to seal the deal. Now Celia has popped up out of nowhere. What am I going to do?"

"Tell Melody how you feel," Javier advised.

"How? I was the one who said I was interested in being friends only. She is going to be –"

"Furious." Javier finished his sentence.

"That's not the exact word that came to mind, but the sentiment is the same."

"Yep, she will be. But you may eventually get forgiven and have a chance. If you don't say anything, you will definitely lose her."

Miguel sighed heavily.

"One more word of advice," Javier offered.

He looked up at his cousin. "Yes, Oprah."

"Don't try to justify your actions or make excuses for

yourself. Admit that you have been wrong and throw yourself on the mercy of the court."

"Javi, can't you give me advice like a regular guy?"

"Isn't it guy thinking that has you where you are?"

MELODY'S PATIO light came on at almost the same time as Miguel's. He decided to let the conversation dictate whether to mention Celia. The most important thing was to find out the status of her relationship with Jesse.

"Hey, Mel."

"Hey, Mig."

For the first time in two years of their patio talks, he felt awkward. Melody was shuffling her feet and appeared restless. He walked over and stood in front of her.

"How was your day? You had a lot of classes, then had to meet with your advisor. Hope it wasn't too hectic."

"Jesse asked me to be his valentine," she blurted out. "I can barely remember the last time I had a boyfriend on Valentine's Day," she said with a nervous laugh.

She looked up at him with glistening eyes and bit her lip. He had to reign in his thoughts about her lips and focus on the conversation.

"So, you told him yes?" The words burned his mouth like acid.

"Well," she started shuffling her feet again, "not yet."

Hope began to bubble in his chest. "Why not?"

"We've only known each other for a week. Isn't that kind of fast? But maybe not. I'm 28. He's 30. Surely, we can tell when it's right. Don't you think?" Her words were rushed, tumbling out of her mouth on top of each other.

"What do you think? Is he the right man for you?" He held his breath, waiting for her answer.

She broke their eye contact and began to pace. Then she stopped moving and faced him.

"I think he could be."

What about me? was on the tip of his tongue, but he couldn't force the words out. Earlier, he'd been so sure about moving forward with her. But now he was faltering. His hope bubble burst. Melody broke the silence.

"Well, I'm going to head back inside. Like you said. It's been a long day. Good night, Miguelito."

His head snapped to attention. "What did you call me?'"

"Miguelito." Her brow furrowed in confusion.

"I'm not a child, Melody. I'm a grown man. And no man wants to be referred to as small or little in any context."

A red blush leaped to her cheeks. "I ... I didn't mean ..."

"I know you weren't trying to insult me, Mel. But sometimes, because I'm your friend, you forget that I'm a man."

MELODY RUSHED INSIDE AS SOON as Miguel turned to go home. His words rang in her ears as she paced her bedroom floor. *You forget that I'm a man.* Nothing could be further from the truth. *He* was the one who didn't think of *her* as a woman. At least not a woman worth dating. Seeing him with Celia confirmed that. She had a decision to make. Either move forward with Jesse who was all in or be satisfied with a friends-only relationship with Miguel that consumed all of her time and her heart. The right choice was becoming more obvious to her by the minute.

MIGUEL LEANED against his patio door disappointed in himself. He'd chickened out on telling Melody how he felt. Then he snapped at her out of frustration.

When he walked out on Celia at lunch, he'd known what he wanted. But though he hated to admit it, seeing Celia had brought old feelings to the surface. However, the memories didn't sting as much.

His resolve returned even stronger than before. He wouldn't let the past or fear hold him back anymore. He'd had a minor setback, but he was determined to fight for Melody. No more being passive. It was time to act. He nodded his head as he formulated his plan. And he had to do it quickly. Valentine's Day was in six days.

CHAPTER ELEVEN

"SHANI, WHAT DO I DO?"

Melody was drained. She'd had a brutally honest conversation with herself over the previous two days. Straddling the fence was tiring. She'd been trying to see where the relationship with Jesse could go while keeping her relationship with Miguel the same. But that wouldn't be fair to Jesse or herself. Her claims of being too busy to date were, truthfully, her hoping and waiting for Miguel. She couldn't think about it anymore. She needed outside help. Now, sprawled across her bed, she sought counsel from her closest friend.

"Mel, it's Friday night, and I'm at home talking to you. If I can't sort out my own love life, how can I help yours?"

"C'mon, Shani. You've never been shy with your opinion or advice." She toyed with the edge of her comforter as her stomach quivered, awaiting Shanice's response.

"Okay, here it is. If you truly believe nothing is ever going to happen with Miguel ..."

"I do," she said confidently. She didn't like it, but it was reality.

"Then you need to let go of the fantasy and move on. Whether Jesse is the person you want to move forward with is something only you can answer. Just don't use him as a pawn."

It was the same conclusion she had come to. A small part of her was hoping that Shanice would see something she was missing. After all, Shanice had always been Team Miguel. But the larger, more practical side of her was glad to be stepping off the emotional rollercoaster.

"Thanks, sis."

"You okay?" Shanice asked with concern.

A sense of peace washed over her, and she sat up. "Yeah, I am." She nodded her head in disbelief that she really was okay. *I guess all I needed was to just make the decision.* "Believe me, I'm as surprised as you are." She smiled and laughed lightly. "Shani, I have to go. Talk to you later."

Melody ended the call with Shanice and immediately placed another one.

"Hello, Jesse? Yes, I will be your Valentine."

~

MIGUEL KNEW he was cutting it close. It was Sunday, the day before Valentine's Day, and he still hadn't talked with Mel. He wasn't procrastinating. The gift he wanted to get for her had been very hard to find, especially with his compressed timeline. It had just been delivered. He'd paid extra – a lot extra – for a Sunday delivery. But, if things went as he hoped, it would all be worth it. He prayed and then called Melody.

"Miguel, what's up?"

Her voice made him smile.

"You free? I want to stop by for a moment."

She laughed. "Since when do you ask? Of course, you can come by."

He was about to make a comment about Jesse then squashed the thought. This wasn't about Jesse. It was about him and Melody.

"Great. I'll be there in a few."

MELODY REFUSED to acknowledge how good Miguel looked or how good he smelled when he came through the door. He stopped in the front room. Normally, he would come all the way in and sit on the couch in front of the television.

"So, *que pasa*?" Melody smiled and sat on the loveseat. Miguel continued to stand.

"I have something for you." He took a small box out of his pocket and handed it to her.

Her curiosity was piqued. "What did you do?"

"Open it." He nudged her knee with his.

She slowly unwrapped the box trying to figure out what it could be at the same time.

"Stop trying to guess what it is and just open it."

She looked up at a smiling Miguel. "How did you know I was –?"

"Your brow always furrows when you're doing your heavy thinking," he said pointing to her forehead.

"Whatever."

Melody finished unwrapping the box and then gently lifted the lid. She gasped. One hand flew to her neck. The other trembled as she stared at the contents of the box. Inside were the matching stud earrings to her gold cross.

Her grandparents gave her the set for her quinceañera. She lost the earrings her sophomore year in college. She had tried on several occasions to replace them, but Abuelo Carlos and Abuela Juanita had bought them in Mexico when she was born. The designer had passed away before they were even given to her. Tears filled her eyes.

"Oh, Miguel!"

She jumped up, wrapped him in a hug, and kissed him on the cheek. Then she came to herself and quickly released him.

"I'm so sorry!" She backed away from him. "I just ... I

have been searching for these for years. I didn't think I'd ever get my set back."

"I know." His eyes smoldered, and his voice was an octave lower.

"I can't believe you remembered! I can't believe you found them! I just ... it was just an automatic reaction," she rushed to explain.

"No need to apologize." He closed the distance she'd put between them in two long, fluid strides. "It was quite nice. In fact, ..."

Miguel encircled her waist with his arm, pulled her to him, and brought his lips to hers.

It was a slow, drugging kiss. Everything but the two of them melted away. His lips caressed hers persuasively. She yielded to their command and opened her mouth to him. He deepened the kiss and shivers raced through her. Her knees begin to buckle. She grabbed handfuls of his shirt to steady herself. Then her eyes flew open.

I'm kissing Miguel! Miguel! We're just friends! We shouldn't be doing this! And I'm with Jesse now!

Melody flattened her palms to his chest and pushed away. She felt a chill once the contact was broken. They stood staring at each other, their chests heaving and hearts pounding.

"What was that?" she asked between breaths.

He chuckled. "If I have to tell you, I wasn't doing it right."

"You know what I mean, Miguel. Why did you kiss me?"

He reached out and took one of her hands in his. "Because I love you and want to be with you."

The room began to spin. She snatched her hand out of his grasp.

"*You what?!?*"

CHAPTER TWELVE

"I love you, Mel. As more than a friend. I want us to be together as a couple. A real couple." Miguel held his breath and waited for her answer.

Melody shook her head. "No."

Not the response he was looking for. "I have wanted to be with you this whole time," he explained.

She folded her arms across her chest. "No."

"I believe we can be good together." He wouldn't give up.

"No," she said through clenched teeth.

"Mel, we know each other. We enjoy each other's company. We respect each other. We're friends." He had to make her see.

"No! We were never friends!" She stepped closer and pointed at him. "You have been lying to me for two years! Friends don't do that!"

"It wasn't so much as lying as not telling you every ..."

Her glare stopped him mid-sentence. He recalled Javier's advice. No justifying. No excuses.

He backtracked. "Yeah, you're right. That's just splitting hairs. I haven't been completely truthful with you," he admitted.

"And why weren't you?" Her voice was hard, and her fists were clenched.

It was the one question he had hoped she wouldn't ask. But if he wanted any chance of being with her, he had to tell the full, ugly truth.

"Because I was protecting myself. We were spending most of our time together anyway. I could have you without having to risk my heart."

She stared at him, mouth open and eyes filled with anger.

Miguel ran his hand through his hair. *This is not going as planned. How can I salvage this?*

"Look. I know it was messed up. It was unfair and selfish and dishonest and every other word that is running through your mind right now. Even the ones you won't allow yourself to say. But I'm putting everything on the table. I'm not holding back anymore. I want to be with you, Mel, and I'm willing to fight for you and do whatever I need to do to make it right."

He prayed she would hear his heart. He couldn't lose her.

"No."

"Mel ..."

"No. This is just the other side of the same coin, Miguel. You decided that we would just be friends. Now, you're deciding that we can be more than friends. As if I don't have a say!" she exclaimed with irritation and frustration.

He shook his head and waved his hands vigorously. "That's not what I meant. I ..."

"The only reason you're saying anything now is because of Jesse. If not for him, you would just continue to monopolize my time and get what you want without any consideration for me and what I want." Her voice and body trembled.

He was silent. Had his fear of being betrayed turned him into the betrayer?

"What? No rebuttal?" she spat out.

He took deep breaths to clear the lump in his throat.

"I know I was wrong, Mel. There's no excuse. You're right. It was all about protecting myself while still getting what I wanted. I have been hugely unfair to you. And I'm asking you to forgive me. Please, forgive me. Please."

He didn't care that he was begging. His future was at stake.

For the first time, she didn't say no.

"Please. I want and need you in my life. Even if you decide you don't want something more, I don't want to lose you as a friend. You're too important to me. You mean too much to me. Please, Mel. Please," Miguel choked out.

"I don't know. Please leave." Her voice was cold and empty.

He reached for her hand, but she jerked it out of reach.

"Don't touch me. I don't want to see you, talk to you, or be around you, right now."

She grabbed the earrings off the loveseat and thrust the box toward him. "Here, take these with you."

He held up both hands. "Those are yours. Do whatever you want with them, but I'm not taking them back."

MIGUEL SLOWLY LICKED his lips as he trudged the short distance from Melody's front door to his, savoring the feel and taste that was uniquely Melody. He'd always thought she'd be passionate because of her caring and dedicated nature. But hadn't been prepared for how deeply he'd be affected. He'd been forever changed by her kiss. And he wanted more. Hundreds of millions more.

Melody had no idea that she'd made him hers.

Even though he'd said he was willing to go back to being friends, his heart wouldn't let him. But she wanted nothing to do with him. He'd gone from experiencing the most amazing sensation he'd ever felt with dreams of forever to pleading to keep Melody in his life. How had it gone so wrong?

Miguel walked into the house and flopped down on the sofa with a heavy sigh.

"By the look on your face I'm guessing things did not go well," Javier said from the recliner.

"Not at all. She ripped me a new one." He dropped his head back and stared at the ceiling.

"Hmm. You liked it, didn't you?

He smiled despite himself. "It was kinda hot. Would have been hotter if it was directed at someone else."

"Granted," Javier said with a nod.

"That and she never wants to see me again."

"Did she say that?"

"Not in those exact words, but context clues made it clear. She is royally P.O.ed."

"You expected her to fall into your arms?" Javier asked in disbelief.

"Well, yeah, kinda," he admitted. "I mean, I expected her to be mad for a moment. But with the earrings and telling her that I love her, I thought she'd get over it and forgive me." He shrugged.

Javier shook his head. "Dude, what is wrong with you? You're acting as if you've never been in a relationship before!"

"Augh!! I know! I just ... I just want back what we had ... plus some."

"If you keep thinking stupid stuff like that it's never gonna happen. You need an intervention."

"Seriously?"

"Clearly, you have no idea how to win her back. So, we need to gather the think tank and come up with some ideas." Javier grabbed his phone off the coffee table.

"This is not one of those chick flicks your sister drags you to. Man, Eliana needs to get more friends. She's ruining you."

Miguel dropped his head in his hands. He could not believe this was happening.

"Probably. But that doesn't negate the fact that you need to do something. Call Rashaad. He's a therapist," Javier suggested.

"You know all he's going to say is 'What do you think you need to do?'" he said imitating their friend.

"Okay, then let's cut to the chase. What do you think you need to do?"

Miguel considered the question. "I need to show her that I meant what I said. I have to put my heart on the line."

CHAPTER THIRTEEN

MELODY WAS SITTING in the same spot she'd been in since Miguel left trying to process what had just happened.

Miguel kissed me! Miguel loves me? Miguel loves me!

She was angry, shocked, and something else she couldn't quite name. Should she ... could she take a chance on Miguel?

He was so insistent on being just friends for two years. And just like that, he wants more? What if he changes his mind again?

She got up and started pacing.

What if Miguel is being driven only by testosterone-fueled competition? What happens when Jesse is out of the picture? I call things off with Jesse, Miguel no longer feels the pressure, and I end up right back where I started. Alone.

Spending time with Jesse had been nice. She didn't

want to be alone anymore. She wanted companionship and romance and a relationship.

She needed to talk to her girls. She sent a 911 text. The phone rang five minutes later.

"Mel, are you okay? What happened?" Sofia asked with concern.

"Miguel told me he loves me."

They all spoke at once. "I knew it!" "What?" "No way!"

"Start from the beginning and don't leave anything out," Shanice ordered.

She relayed the events of the afternoon alternating between English and Spanish. A range of emotions coursed through her words and soul.

"What are you going to do?" Carmen asked

She decided at that moment.

"Stick to my plan. I'm going to dinner with Jesse and starting a real relationship with him," she said resolutely.

"Really?" Shanice asked.

"Yes, really," she insisted. "Now that someone else has stepped up and wants to be with me, all of a sudden Miguel does a 180? Now he makes a profession of love? It's a little too coincidental for me."

She continued to rant. Her friends listened silently.

"Not to mention that he was very cozy with Celia less than a week ago!" she said drawing her tirade to a close.

"That could have been nothing," Sofia said.

"If it was nothing, he would have told me about it,"

she countered. "But it doesn't matter. I've made up my mind. I'm going to be with Jesse."

"That's your mind. What is your heart saying?" Shanice asked.

MIGUEL PERIODICALLY LOOKED out his front window on Valentine's Day. Melody hadn't spoken to him since his confession, but he knew she was most likely going to spend time with Jesse. When he saw a sleek, black sedan pass his house and pull into Melody's driveway around 6:00 PM, he decided to check his mail. A tall man got out and lifted his hand in a friendly wave.

"You must be Miguel."

"You must be Jesse."

Jesse walked over. The two men shook hands and sized each other up. Miguel grudgingly acknowledged that some might consider Jesse moderately attractive.

"We saw you at Abbott's the other day, but didn't want to interrupt your date."

His stomach dropped. *Oh great. Melody saw me with Celia.*

"It wasn't a date. Just a meeting with a former acquaintance," he corrected him.

Jesse nodded silently while looking at Miguel with curiosity as if he knew his secret. Miguel didn't like it.

"So, are you two heading out to dinner?" He asked,

hoping to draw Jesse into a conversation and make him late. Melody hated tardiness.

"We are. And we have a reservation, so I better get going." Jesse began walking up Melody's driveway. "Enjoy the rest of your Valentine's Day," he said with a wave.

Miguel rolled his neck and shoulders to release the tension that had built up in the past five minutes.

"Yeah, thanks. I will. Oh, make sure she doesn't get anything with cinnamon. She's allergic."

"I'm sure Melody ...," Jesse started then stopped himself. "I'll be sure not to. Thanks for the heads up."

Jesse rang Melody's doorbell and then disappeared into her house through the opened door.

"You seemed kind of distracted tonight. Is everything okay?" Jesse asked Melody on their way back to her house from dinner and a string quartet performance.

Melody had tried to hide it, but the incident with Miguel on Sunday afternoon had been playing in her mind non-stop. Evidently, she hadn't succeeded.

"I just have a lot on my mind. I'm sorry if I wasn't the best company. I did enjoy myself. The concert was a nice surprise." She smiled at him. Jesse was a great guy.

"Can I ask you a frank question?" He kept his eyes on the road.

"Of course. How can we build this relationship if we aren't willing to be open with each other?"

Jesse nodded and tapped the steering wheel with his fingers.

"What's your relationship with Miguel?"

"He's my neighbor and my friend." She kept her voice even, but her insides were jumping.

"Just friends? That's all it has ever been? You never dated?" His voice was slightly strained, and his expression was clouded.

"No. Why?"

"Because he likes you. Probably loves you."

Melody felt her cheeks warm and a film of sweat arise on her chest.

"What makes you say that?"

He glanced at her with a half-smile. "You didn't deny it."

"Jesse, what Miguel does or doesn't feel has nothing to do with you and me," she insisted as he turned into her subdivision.

"That would be true if you didn't have feelings for him."

He pulled into her driveway, then turned the car off and shifted in his seat to face her.

"Melody, I really like you. I can see a future with you. But I don't want to be your second choice."

"Jesse, I don't have–"

"At best you're unsure," he interrupted. "You can't

start a relationship with me when you're unsure about another man."

Jesse got out and walked around to the other side of the car. He helped her out and clasped her hand in his as he walked her to her front door.

"I'm going to give you time to sort this out." She opened her mouth to argue, but he held up his hand. "If I'm wrong – I hope I am, but I don't think I am – call me. You have my number."

He kissed her chastely on the forehead and left.

Melody stood on her porch until she could no longer see the tail lights of Jesse's car. She was stunned and numb, unable to make sense of what had happened. Then she was overwhelmed with a barrage of emotions, too many coming at her too fast for her to identify them all. She closed her eyes and vigorously shook her head hoping to wake herself up from a bad dream. But when she opened her eyes, everything was the same. It was her reality.

Her body began to tremble. She rushed inside and quickly shut the door. The last thing she needed was for her neighbors to witness her having a breakdown.

Leaning against her front door, she took inventory of the current situation. *When did I land in the twilight zone?* For the second time in two days, a man in her life flipped the script, upending everything she thought she knew about the nature and future of her relationship with him. Jesse, who essentially asked her to be his girlfriend less than a week ago, just bowed out of her life. Miguel, who had insisted they be just friends for two years, wanted them to be a couple. *What is going on? And what do I do now?*

The weight of her situation became tangible, causing her to slide down the door until she was sitting on the floor. In her cute dress and designer heels. She opened her mouth to give herself a pep talk, but instead of words, sobbing poured out, and tears streamed down her face.

CHAPTER FOURTEEN

Miguel sent Melody another text, hoping she was not blocking him.

Me: *Good morning. I know you'll teach a great class this month, Doc. You always do.*

"Nice. Shows her you remembered what day she's teaching and that you're thinking of her," Javier said from over his shoulder.

Miguel tossed his phone on the couch with a sigh.

"I wonder if I'm wasting my time. That's the tenth text I've sent in the past week. Still no response."

"Give her time, Mig. You dropped a bomb on her."

"I know. I'm not giving up. It's just ... I did what I had been avoiding for two years. Apparently, I was right. Because as soon as I risked my heart again, exactly what I thought would happen happened. The rug was pulled out from under me. Now, there's no way back to where we were and no indication of a future."

He put his elbows on his knees and dropped his head into his hands. Melody was right next door yet miles away.

"If you really feel that way, why are you still texting her, leaving her messages, and going out on your patio every night?" Javier challenged.

"Because I know in my heart we're meant to be."

"Then you have to have faith, brother. Don't let what you see trick you into giving up on what you know."

MELODY CLOCKED out of her overnight shift and debated whether to use the tiny box the hospital called a shower or go home. She decided to take her chances in the locker room. If she hurried, she might be the only one there and could have some privacy. Going home would make her think of Miguel. Not that she wasn't already. But it would be worse at home with all the reminders of him.

Her phone dinged with another text message.

"Speak of the ..." Her eyes watered as she read.

She had read every text and listened to every voicemail he'd sent her over the past week at least five times. But she avoided seeing him. Her life consisted of school and work. She picked up more shifts, not for the money or the experience, but to make sure she was exhausted once she finally got home and would fall into a dreamless sleep. Whatever it took to avoid more dreams of Miguel and his mind-blowing kiss. She hadn't even talked to her girls since her tearful recounting of how her Valentine's Day had ended. Jesse wouldn't tell her what, if anything, Miguel said or did, but she still blamed him for sabotaging her evening and her budding relationship with Jesse.

Even though she was angry with Miguel, she still cared about him and liked that he was pursuing her. And that made her angry with herself. *Why can't I just shake him loose and move on with my life? I need an intervention.*

"WE WERE GIVING you until the end of today before we were going to show up at your house," Shanice said.

"*Si*. I was looking at flights, and Carmen reserved a rental car," Sofia added.

"How are you?" Carmen asked.

Melody let out a humorless laugh. "Not good. I've been burying myself in work and school, but ignoring Miguel hasn't changed the way that I feel."

"How do you feel?" Shanice asked.

She thought for a moment then let what she had been holding in pour out of her. "I feel played. I feel like I have been strung along. I feel disregarded. But at the same time, I'm miserable without him, and I'm mad at myself for that. But mostly, I'm angry – really angry – with Miguel." The tension in her neck and shoulders eased slightly.

"Then tell him," Shanice advised. "You're not going to be able to come to any kind of resolution until you do."

MIGUEL STOOD at his patio door with his hand hovering over the light switch.

"No response to or even acknowledgment of any of my messages. No patio conversations. The last time I saw her was when she was leaving with Jesse for their date a week ago. Am I a complete idiot or a man of faith?" He asked himself aloud.

The answer didn't come from his mind but from his spirit. "I'm a man of faith. How can I expect her to believe me and see that I am putting my heart out there if I can't last past a week?"

Certainty took root in him. He smiled a genuine smile for the first time since he confessed his love to her. He and Melody were going to be together for the rest of their lives. This wasn't going to be the last time she was mad at him. He turned on the light and went outside.

MELODY WAS LYING DIAGONALLY across her bed looking up at the ceiling, but her mind was replaying the conversation with her girls. They were right. She needed to act like the grown woman she was and tell Miguel how she felt. Just then, light peeked through the half-closed blinds of the window that faced Miguel's townhouse.

"No time like the present."

Melody hoisted herself off the bed, walked through her sunroom, flipped on her patio light, and stepped outside.

MIGUEL WAS SITTING in one of his patio chairs when Melody's light came on. He heard her door open and leaped to his feet.

"Hi," she said from the center of her patio.

"Hi." He couldn't help but smile. *This is a good thing, right?* "I'm glad you came out tonight."

She didn't respond.

"Does this mean you forgive me?"

"Yes. I forgive you."

His smile grew wider. *This night could not be bet-*

"But ..." His smile faltered. "But I'm not ready to just pick up where we left off ... or beyond that."

"Mel ..."

She shook her head. "No, listen. You know me. You know I analyze and reanalyze and then analyze some more. The thing that concerns me most is not that you didn't tell me that you had feelings for me. It's why you didn't tell me. And it's not because Celia hurt you."

"Uh, it's not?"

"No."

"Could have fooled me," he muttered under his breath.

She walked toward the edge of her patio. He moved to the edge of his.

"If that were the real reason, you would have held your peace," she asserted.

He started to disagree but decided to listen and hear her out.

"Because not wanting to risk being hurt again would have outweighed your discomfort of seeing me with Jesse."

He considered her words. *Could she be right?*

"It's about what you think you have a right to. What you consider yours. I'm not property, Miguel. My time, my energy, and my attention are mine. And I give them to whom I choose."

He dropped his head. What she said wasn't incorrect, but it was incomplete. But it was not the time to argue.

"I understand, Mel. And I'm not just saying that to get back in your good graces, although I do want to get back into your good graces. I'm owning up to what I did. I'm committed to being open and honest. I'm not giving up on us."

He looked at her across the small patch of grass that

separated them. It was the closest he'd been to her since their kiss. The kiss that had been keeping him up for the past week. Begging for a repeat. How was that going to happen when he couldn't even get her to sit on his patio?

Melody started backing away, but he could tell she was considering what he said. She turned to leave.

"I miss you, Mel."

She turned back to face him. "I miss you, too." She held his gaze for a brief moment then went inside.

He waited until he heard her patio door lock and her light turned off. Then he pumped his fist in the air and whispered "YES!!"

CHAPTER FIFTEEN

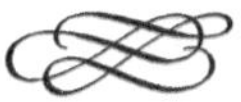

"YOU SOUND MUCH BETTER today than you did a week ago," Shanice said.

Melody walked her bedroom floor while she talked to Shanice. Not pacing out of worry, but moving with excitement and energy she hadn't felt in over two weeks.

"Yeah," she said nodding. "You were right. Once I told him how I felt, it cleared the way for us to at least be in each other's presence."

"Really? How so?"

She could hear the smile in Shanice's voice. But then, she was smiling, too.

"Well, we've had a few patio talks. Miguel cooked dinner twice this past week, and both times he sent a container home with me for lunch the next day. He put up motion sensor flood lights outside the garage and at my front door. But the kicker was on Saturday."

"What did he do on Saturday that outshines quality time, feeding you, and making your place safer?"

"He joined me for my morning run." *Mic drop.*

"What?"

"This is the first time in the two years we have known each other that he ran with me. He came out right when I got to the end of my driveway. He was dressed and ready to go. Had his music and everything. He must have gotten up early, dressed, and waited for me to come out." She shook her head, still finding it hard to believe that he had done that.

"Didn't he say the only type of run he had ever done was a beer run?" Shanice asked.

Melody laughed. "Yes, he did."

"All that in a week? Hmm. He sounds like a man on a mission."

She had enjoyed spending time with Miguel the past week, but she couldn't squelch the voice that was telling her she was setting herself up again. She needed to proceed with caution.

"Maybe. But, Shani, I can't let myself get caught up in the good feelings, and ... Oh, he just turned his light on. Gotta go!"

Before she hung up, she heard Shanice say, "Girl, you need to stop the madness and ..."

MIGUEL WAS FEELING GOOD. Things were better between him and Melody. Most evenings in the past week, she came out to talk but stayed on her patio. He chuckled as he recalled the look on her face when he joined her on her Saturday run. He'd paid for that gesture, though. It was Tuesday, and he was still sore. Things were better, but she would only call him Miguel. What he wouldn't give to hear her call him Mig or Miggy. It was a small thing, but it mattered to him.

He turned on the light and sat down in one of his patio chairs. Soon after, he looked to his left and saw Melody walking over. He was rendered motionless. His brain was telling him to stand up to receive her, but his legs wouldn't move. By the time he finally connected his mind and body and started to get up, she took the chair next to him and began talking about her day. He tried to remain calm and focus on what she was saying, but his heart was doing somersaults.

Melody rubbed her arms.

"You want to come inside? It's a little chilly. I know you don't like to be cold," he offered.

"Sure," she said with a shrug.

She followed him inside and continued talking. They were standing face-to-face when she finished her update. She was in his house, looking up at him, less than five feet away. He decided to take the opportunity that had been given to him.

"Why didn't you tell me about your first date with Jesse?"

The stunned look on her face told him his question was unexpected.

"I ... I... I don't know," she stammered.

"Yes, you do. Why didn't you tell me?"

"Because ... because," She let out a heavy sigh and closed her eyes for a moment. When she opened them, she looked as if she was weighing whether to answer him. "Because it felt wrong to tell you. I felt ... guilty for some reason," she blurted out.

"Because you knew," he said taking a measured step forward.

She remained silent and still.

"You knew that even though we denied it to others, we knew in ourselves that we are more than friends. Much more than friends. I belong to you, and you belong to me."

MELODY'S HEAD WAS SWIMMING. When Miguel said they belonged to each other, her heart vehemently agreed, but she wasn't ready to admit it aloud. Before she could formulate a response, he spoke again.

"Have you kissed him?"

She had not. She hadn't even seen or spoken to Jesse

since Valentine's Day. But she wasn't about to tell him either of those things.

"Miguel, I am not answering that question. You have no right to ask that, and I have no obligation to answer you." She spoke with much more composure than she felt.

He grinned and began to slowly walk toward her. "I'm going to take that as a no. *Solo yo, mi amor? Si?* I'm the only man you have kissed in two years. *Esta bein?*"

With his every advance, she retreated until she made contact with the wall. He was as close to her as he could be without touching her. But the effect was the same. He had invaded her space, and the sliver of air between them was so charged it felt like they were pressed together.

"Oh, and I have every right to ask," he continued in a husky voice. "You belong to me, remember?"

"I don't belong to anyone, remember?" She attempted a defiant tone.

"*Al contratio.* You're my wife, Mel. You're the mother of my children. My life partner. But I can wait for your head to realize what your heart already knows."

Miguel moved back just enough for her to step around him. Melody brushed against him as she made her exit and shivered at the contact.

CHAPTER SIXTEEN

"An emergency lunch call, Mel? Really?" Carmen asked.

"Yes," Melody whispered. She was the only person in the graduate student lounge at the time, but the walls had ears. She didn't want the entire College of Allied Health to know her business.

"I'm assuming this is about Miguel. Go ahead and catch us up," Sofia said.

After Melody relayed the previous night's events – edited a bit – she waited for their response.

"Maybe I missed something," Carmen sounded puzzled. "Is the question what you should wear to meet him tonight?"

"No! I'm trying to sort through whether to move forward with him. He played me for two years!" she insisted, but honestly, she wasn't as upset as when she first found out.

"I think 'played' is a bit harsh. And you were a willing participant and recipient in that semi-relationship," Sofia asserted.

Sofia was right. At any time, she could have set boundaries or pulled back. She had played a part and received benefits. Her argument was quickly losing steam and validity.

"And you're not denying that you love him," Shanice challenged.

It would have been a lie if she did.

"Then it's unanimous. The council has decided. Swallow any pride and hurt feelings from the past and embrace your future with Miguel," Carmen announced.

Melody sighed and smiled, but evidently, she was too slow in responding for Shanice.

"Girl, you have wanted that man for two years. Quit playin' and go get him!"

MIGUEL WALKED into his sunroom wondering whether he had come on too strong with Melody the night before. His internal dialogue halted when he saw her patio light come on. She had beat him to it! He rushed over and caught her coming out the door, one foot in her sunroom and one on the patio. He wrapped both arms around her waist and pulled her to him. He held off from kissing her. He didn't want to make any assumptions. She looked up at him, her eyes sparkling with humor. And she was wearing the earrings!

"Well, hello to you, too." She ran her hands up his arms and clasped them behind his neck.

"So does this mean ...?" He wanted – needed – her to complete the sentence.

"Yes. I want to be with you as more than friends. Much more than friends. Because, I love you, too, Miggy."

His heart leaped. His lips crashed down on hers, and he claimed her for himself. Minutes later their mouths separated, but he held her in his embrace.

"I knew we were meant to be together," he said between heavy breaths. "We have the same initials."

Melody laughed. "Miguel Martinez, we do not!"

"Maybe not now, but we will."

CHAPTER SEVENTEEN

MAY of the Next Year

The last of the guests were milling around Miguel's great room. Melody, still in her doctoral gown, hood, and tam, closed the front door behind a group of cousins who were heading to Javier's house for the afterparty.

She leaned against the front door and took in the sight before her. The custom-made banner saying "Congratulations, Dr. Melody J. Correra" hung above the fireplace, balloon clusters stood in every corner, streamers were draped along the crown molding, and confetti was scattered on every table.

Melody released a contented sigh. The day had been perfect. And all she had to do was show up. Her gaze fell to Miguel, causing a warm feeling to spread through her chest. He'd insisted on hosting the graduation party at his place, saying that Melody had enough to do with pre-graduation activities and the graduation itself. That she shouldn't have to think about cleaning and preparing for guests. And that he *wanted* to do it for her.

She smiled at the memory of their mothers' reactions when she and Miguel talked about using a caterer for the party. They'd hit the roof and been adamant that they would cook. It turned out for the best. The food had been amazing, and the mothers were able to share the kitchen and get along. As Shanice, Sofia, and Carmen put away leftovers and cleaned the kitchen, the moms sat on the sofa laughing, talking, and sneaking glances at her and Miguel. Melody shook her head. They were probably planning out their children's lives for the next 30 years.

She still didn't know how, but Miguel had miraculously convinced everyone, even their parents, to stay somewhere other than at her house or his. So, when the last of the family and friends said goodbye, it was just the two of them.

Melody pulled off her graduate regalia and gently laid them across the arm of the chair in the front room. Then she leaned against the wall of the archway and exhaled.

"You okay?" Miguel looked up from collapsing and stacking folding chairs.

"Yeah. It's been a long day, and I'm tired. But it's a good tired."

She couldn't stop smiling. She adored Miguel and was so grateful to have him as her friend and her love. She crossed the room, took a chair out of his hand then leaned it against the sofa.

Pulling him into a tight embrace, she whispered, "Thank you. For everything. I love you."

He squeezed her even tighter. "I love you, too." He pulled back some but kept his arms around her. "How about a patio talk?"

Guests had started arriving four days before graduation. Between airport pick-ups, entertaining company, and preparing for the party, they hadn't had time alone in almost a week. "That sounds wonderful. Your place or mine?"

THEY SETTLED into the chairs on Miguel's patio. It was early evening, so the sun was still out but not blazing overhead. A soft, late spring breeze blew through the trees.

"So, how does it feel?"

"Wonderful!" Melody lifted her hands in the air and then leaned back, relaxing in the chair. "It's the payoff for all the work, time, and effort. And I got my first choice for my post-doc program."

"Uh, and me!" he reminded her.

She laughed and placed her hand on his cheek. "Yes, Miggy, you most of all. You've been so wonderful I ... I don't know what to say."

"How about 'yes'?"

She was confused until he got out of the chair and went down on one knee. Her hands flew to her face as he pulled a ring box out of his pocket and flipped it open.

"Dr. Melody Juanita Correra, will you marry me?"

"Oh, Miguel! YES!"

MIGUEL, grinning widely, gently pulled her left hand away from her cheek and slid the diamond solitaire ring on her finger. For a few moments, they remained in those positions. Miguel on one knee holding her hand. Melody seated in the chair smiling with love shining in her eyes through happy tears. Sealing that moment in time into their memories forever.

Then Melody launched herself out of the chair and into Miguel's arms. The force of the unexpected contact caused him to topple over and land on his back, taking her with him. She, unfazed by the change in position, showered him with kisses. They stayed that way for hours, laughing, kissing, declaring their love, and planning their future together.

A year and a half prior, Melody didn't think she would ever find love. But love was right next door all the time.

Present Day...

"AND HERE WE ARE, married for 20 years with a 16-year-old and a 14-year-old," Melody told Kristen as the server cleared the dessert plates.

"Wow, that's quite a story! And very sweet." Kristen grinned. "But none of that applies to me, Mel. I don't have a great guy as a friend who is secretly in love with me. And even if I did, it wouldn't matter. I've learned the hard way not to expect fairytale, romance novel, or rom-com movie endings. My life is good. And a relationship just isn't in the plan for me. That's why I stick to my rules," she said firmly.

"I know you have dating rules, Kristen. And I'm not saying that my exact story will be yours. I'm just saying, love can turn up in the most unexpected places."

ABOUT THE AUTHOR

Marie Hobbs is an avid reader and emerging author of inspirational romance. She has been creating stories in her mind even before she could write. She credits her mother for her love of reading and writing. Her mother encouraged reading, writing, and creativity by reading bedtime stories to her and her siblings, taking her to library book sales, and walking with her to the bookmobile in the summer. Now, Marie has the opportunity to share stories that will encourage, inspire, and entertain others the way she was.

For more information visit www.mariehobbs.com.